The

Grumpy
Gnome

Goes on Holiday

Written and illustrated by
Della Jayne Hales

Matador
9 Priory Business Park,
Wistow Road, Kibworth Beauchamp,
Leicestershire. LE8 0RX
Tel: 0116 279 2299
Email: books@troubador.co.uk
Web: www.troubador.co.uk/matador
Twitter: @matadorbooks

ISBN 978 1800463 431

British Library Cataloguing in Publication Data.
A catalogue record for this book is available from the British Library.

Typeset in 12pt Book Antiqua by Troubador Publishing Ltd, Leicester, UK

Matador is an imprint of Troubador Publishing Ltd

Dedicated to:
Rosalie & Poppy
Theodore
Oliver

Many thanks to Dr Gary Tennant
for brushing up my English!

About the Author

Della comes from Hertfordshire and works for a not for profit mediation service.

This is Della's second book, the first being *The Grumpy Gnome's Garden*.

Della's main hobby is crafting, and she always has a project on the go, i.e. greeting cards, children's clothes, furniture restoration, dolls, soft furnishings, needle felting, embroidery, illustrating, etc, etc. Della adores working in her studio situated deep in the heart of Ashridge Forest. Della's craftwork can be viewed on her website:

www.serendipitoustradingcompany.co.uk.

Della loves spending time with her young granddaughters, who often come for a sleepover.

Della enjoys travelling and this book is based on a visit to Le Palais Idéal, near Lyon, in France.

Chapter One

The Grumpy Gnome Goes on Holiday

The Grumpy Gnome worked very hard making things out of wood all day. He rarely took time off to do anything else and had not been on holiday for a long time. Once upon a time he was very lonely and didn't have anything in his life but work to occupy his time.

Things had been very different ever since his friends the Fairy Princess, Captain Robert and First Mate Ron had been visiting. Nowadays, he was friendly with lots of people in the neighbourhood and community. He received an invite to a party or local celebration almost every month!

Scoobit, the Grumpy Gnome's beloved cat, had come to live with him and kept him company. Scoobit liked play fighting with the

Grumpy Gnome and also having his beautiful white fur brushed. All Scoobit's meals were freshly prepared by the Grumpy Gnome and never came from a tin.

The Grumpy Gnome's garden kept him very busy too. Now it had been transformed from a wilderness to a nice space by the Fairy Princess, there were lots of plants that needed watering every day.

He had lots of visitors who came to see his garden, which had become quite famous after the Fairy Princess had made the Apple Fizz and sold it outside the gate.

The Help the Gnomeless charity had even awarded the Grumpy Gnome a medal for all the money he had raised from the sales of the Apple Fizz and then donated!

One weekend, the Fairy Princess came to visit him. She seemed very excited about something.

"I believe it's your birthday soon, Grumpy Gnome. I have planned to go away to France for a few days, and you are coming too," she said.

The Grumpy Gnome opened his mouth to say something, but the Fairy Princess carried on.

"I don't want any excuses or grumpery, you are coming and that's the end of it! It will do you good. I have arranged to visit my good friend, Madame Craccodile of Lyon. We are going to see a famous garden that she told me about. As we all love gardens so much, Marko the Wisp, Captain Robert and First Mate Ron are coming too," she continued.

The Fairy Princess paused and peered at the Grumpy Gnome to see his reaction. He thought for a moment and then asked, "Who will look after the garden and Scoobit whilst we are away?"

"Don't worry about that, I have it all arranged. My friend, the Welsh Dragon, is coming round. She will take care of everything," replied the Fairy Princess.

The Grumpy Gnome couldn't think of any more excuses to get out of going away and reluctantly agreed. When he finally came round to the idea, he started to feel quite excited and even said he would drive there in his car, Miss Morag Minor.

The Fairy Princess had planned to transport them all to Madame Craccodile's with her Fairy Power, but she loved riding in Miss Morag Minor.

Miss Morag Minor was the Grumpy Gnome's pride and joy. She had beautiful sage green paintwork, with a wooden frame. The Grumpy Gnome housed her in his garage tucked up in a woollen tartan rug. He always kept her paintwork and chrome polished and shiny.

The day before they were due to leave, the Welsh Dragon arrived.

"Prynhawn da!" she said as the Fairy Princess greeted her at the door.

"What does that mean?" whispered the Grumpy Gnome looking confused.

"It means 'good afternoon' in Welsh," the Fairy Princess whispered back.

The Welsh Dragon was eccentric (like most of the Fairy Princess' friends). She was dressed in a Welsh tartan kilt, a Welsh rugby shirt and a hat that made her lovely, shaped head look like a daffodil. She wheeled in her suitcase and was carrying two large carrier bags full of Welsh gifts, such as cheese, biscuits, and sweets.

"You shouldn't have, but thank you," said the Fairy Princess giving the Dragon a hug. "We ought to be giving you gifts for helping out!" she added.

"I know how much you like them," said the Dragon softly. "I've also got a catnip toy for Scoobit," she added, dangling a mouse on a stick in front of him. Scoobit immediately caught it with one of his huge pink paws and, biting hard, held it in his mouth.

"We'll have a lot of fun together Scoobit," said the Dragon tickling him behind one of his pink ears. He started to purr, still gripping the toy mouse firmly in his mouth.

They walked around the garden and the Fairy Princess showed the Dragon how to fill, and where to empty, the slug traps. It was late spring and all the plants in the garden (including the weeds!) were very busy sprouting their new shoots. There was plenty of work to do every day to keep the garden maintained.

For dinner, the Grumpy Gnome cooked roast lamb, which as you may know is a baby sheep. It is well known that Welsh people are very fond of sheep and this one had come from Wales, according to the butcher.

"This is lush!" exclaimed Dragon. She ate all the food on her plate. The Fairy Princess could not eat all her food and didn't want to upset the Grumpy Gnome by leaving any. When he wasn't looking, she scraped the food from her plate onto Dragon's. Dragon ate the leftovers and the Grumpy Gnome looked pleased at the empty plates.

Captain Robert and First Mate Ron arrived early the next morning. They were wearing matching red and white stripey tops and French berets. First Mate Ron had drawn thin moustaches on their faces with an eyebrow pencil.

"We thought we'd dress in proper French style," said First Mate Ron, puffing out her chest with pride. Captain Robert just rolled his eyes and said nothing.

Marko-the-Wisp came dashing through the gate carrying an old, battered suitcase. He was wearing a red and white stripey top and a French beret too!

"Snap," squealed First Mate Ron!

They stood looking at each other giggling.

"I don't have a moustache though," said Marko-the-Wisp, eyeing First Mate Ron's upper lip decoration enviously.

"We can soon sort that out," said First Mate Ron, getting her eyebrow pencil out of her bag and licking it. "Hold still while I draw one on you!"

She drew one half of the moustache on Marko-the-Wisp's top lip. Just as she was doing the other half, Marko-the-Wisp sneezed, and the pencil went right across his cheek!

"Oh dear, you're a bit wonky," said First Mate Ron, "But it suits you!"

"Marvellous!", exclaimed Marko-the-Wisp.

The Grumpy Gnome loaded the luggage into the car but there were so many cases and bags that he had to tie some onto the roof. They all said goodbye to Dragon.

Scoobit was nowhere to be found. The Grumpy Gnome felt sad not to have seen him before they left.

Finally, they all got into the car and drove off to the ferry port on the coast.

Dragon went back into the cottage to prepare Scoobit's breakfast. She went out the back and called him, but there was no sign of him.

"Strange," thought Dragon and guessed he must be out hunting somewhere. She fetched the watering can and started to water the thirsty plants.

Chapter Two

France

The holiday party were on their way to the port which was a long journey. First Mate Ron had bought a large tin of sweets which she passed round. The Fairy Princess played her ukulele, and they were all having a singsong. The time passed quickly.

Presently, First Mate Ron shouted, "I can see the sea! Look!" pointing in excitement. They all craned their necks and saw the silver line on the horizon glistening in the sunlight.

They soon reached the ferry port and drove Miss Morag Minor up the gangplank to board the ferry bound for France.

They all went up on deck and watched as the ferry pulled away from the port to begin its voyage. The sea was very calm and there were hardly any waves. Seagulls followed the ferry, crying out as they flew around.

They watched as the port faded further and further into the distance until they could no longer see land.

After a couple of hours of sailing, they reached France.

They waited in the queue of cars to get off the ferry and then drove off down the gangplank.

The Grumpy Gnome said, "I'm hungry".

"So am I," added the Fairy Princess. Everyone else nodded in agreement.

First Mate Ron spotted a little café nearby. "There, that place looks nice," she said. The Grumpy Gnome parked up outside.

"I need to fetch my handbag from the back," said First Mate Ron. She got out of the car and opened the back door. As she reached in to get her bag, she gasped and jumped back!

"We have a stowaway on board!" squealed First Mate Ron, pointing to the back of the car with her mouth wide open. They all dashed around the back of the car and stared inside.

There, stretched out, washing one of his back paws, was Scoobit! He just ignored them staring at him and carried on washing himself.

"We can't turn back now," said the Grumpy Gnome gazing lovingly at Scoobit (who was now washing his other paw). "We'd better get word to the Welsh Dragon, otherwise she will be worried about him," he added.

"Look, there's a souvenir shop across the road, we can get a postcard and send it to her. If we post it first class it will be there by the morning," said First Mate Ron.

Off she went inside the shop and came out a few minutes later looking very pleased clutching a small paper bag containing a postcard of the Eiffel Tower along with a postage stamp.

"Alternatively, we could text her," sighed the Fairy Princess to herself. "She'll know straight away, then!" She sent Dragon a text without First Mate Ron noticing, not wishing to dampen her spirits.

They went in to the café (including Scoobit) and sat down at a table. First Mate Ron wrote out the postcard, added Grumpy Gnome's address and stuck the postage stamp to it.

"Bonjour!" said the waiter, eyeing First Mate Ron, Marko-the-Wisp and Captain Robert in their bizarre 'French' outfits.

"That means 'Hello' in French," whispered the Fairy Princess. "Bonjour!" they all replied back to the waiter, much to his amusement.

The Fairy Princess ordered coffee and croissants for them all, plus some warm milk for Scoobit.

"In France, they dip their croissants in coffee," announced First Mate Ron, dunking her croissant in her coffee before popping it into her mouth.

"Sounds a bit weird!" said Marko-the-Wisp, also dipping his croissant in his coffee. Unfortunately, he left it in there a bit too long and it plopped into the cup! "Oops!" he exclaimed and had to eat the rest of it with a teaspoon.

When they had finished, they paid the bill and left the café. First Mate Ron put the postcard to Dragon in the post box.

They got back into Miss Morag Minor and then drove down towards Lyon. It took several hours but by evening time, they finally reached Madame Craccodile's house.

Madame Craccodile was waiting for them, along with her friend, Nosferatus, and two cats, Babbine and Newt. Babbine was very fat and shy. Newt was curious (even by cat standards!) and circled the room walking around the tops of Madame Craccodile's cupboards, looking down on everyone. They were both pleased to see Scoobit and came to greet him.

Nosferatus was a wonderful chef and he had prepared a meal for them. They had snails in garlic and cream. Then fried frogs' legs, with French bread and cheese. For afters, they had fresh raspberry mousse.

"We will leave early tomorrow morning," said Madame Craccodile. "I have beds ready for you all to sleep in tonight."

They went to their beds, tired from the journey, and all fell asleep almost as their heads touched the pillow.

The next morning, they had a breakfast of bread, cheese, and cold meat.

Then they got ready to set off. Nosferatus, Madame Craccodile, Babbine and Newt were travelling in Nosferatus' old 2CV car.

Nosferatus got in his car and started the engine. It spluttered a bit, then stopped. He tried to start it again and the same thing happened. He wound down the window, leaned his head out and shouted, "Poussez, poussez!"

The Fairy Princess asked Madame Craccodile, "What does 'poussez' mean?"

"It means push!" replied Madame Craccodile wearily.

They got out of Miss Morag Minor and stood behind the old 2CV car. They started to push the car along the road. First, it went slowly, but as they gained momentum, it went faster and faster. They were laughing so much whilst they were pushing that people had stopped in the street to watch the spectacle.

Suddenly, the 2CV sprang into life and chugged off up the road. They were still pushing with all their might and fell flat on their faces in the middle of the road, still laughing helplessly.

Finally, they set off with the 2CV leading the way and Miss Morag Minor following. It was quite a long way to the famous garden and so they had planned to make some stops along the way.

However, there were also some unplanned stops. Nosferatus' 2CV broke down every few miles and they had to keep getting out to 'pousser'.

The third time it broke down, Nosferatus opened the bonnet and peered in scratching his head.

"We're never going to get there at this rate," muttered the Fairy Princess to herself.

Nosferatus had gone to the boot to fetch a spanner. When his back was turned, she took a small pinch of fairy dust out of her bag and blew it all over the engine.

Nosferatus came back and tapped the spanner a couple times on the engine, which wasn't going to achieve anything.

"Bon," he said and got back into the car. He tried the engine and it sounded like a racing car! He sped off up the road at high speed and had to stop after a while to let Miss Morag Minor catch up with them.

Chapter Three

Parc de la Tête d'Or

The first planned stop was Lyon City Park (or the Parc de la Tête d'Or).

The Fairy Princess wanted to take some photos of the red squirrels that she had been told lived there.

The park had botanical glass houses, a small zoo and a large boating lake. They walked round the zoo, looking at the animals for a few hours.

There were lions, tigers, a crocodile pond, giraffes, elephants, and many different types of birds.

As they stood looking at the giraffes, Marko-the-Wisp said, "That one looks very friendly," and gave it a wave. It bent its head over the fence and sniffed Marko-the-Wisp. Then it licked him with its enormous, black tongue covering him in giraffe slobber!

"Eeeeergh!" shrieked Marko-the-Wisp.

First Mate Ron, the Fairy Princess and Madame Craccodile managed to dry him off with some handkerchiefs, but they decided it was a good time to leave the zoo.

As they were coming out of the zoo exit, the Fairy Princess saw a group of red squirrels in a small wood of evergreen trees. She pulled out her camera and slowly stalked over to the squirrels.

As she approached the little group, they all scuttled away up the trees, except for one.

She pointed her camera at the squirrel. He was standing on his hind legs looking at her, almost as if he was posing to have his picture taken. The Fairy Princess clicked the camera, and a message came up on the screen saying, 'memory card full'.

"Oh no!" she exclaimed, "What a time to run out of memory!" She reached into her bag and rummaged around for her spare memory card. She tried to change the cards over, but she was trying to do it so quickly that her hands kept fumbling. All the while the squirrel kept posing!

She finally loaded the spare memory card into the camera and took several pictures of him.

He was such a handsome creature with bright red fur and long tufty ears.

However, he appeared to be quite angry and glared at her almost like he wanted to chase her off! She wished she had some nuts to give him, but only had peppermints which she doubted he would like. She quickly walked away to join the others, delighted with her photos. The squirrel still stood there watching her walk away, possibly wishing she'd had some nuts too.

Following that, they all went to the boating lake and hired three swan shaped paddle boats. They paddled all the way round the edge in a line, one behind the other. The cats didn't want to go in the boats, so just sat in the sunshine on the shore watching them.

When they got back to the jetty they got out of the boats and went to find Scoobit, Babbine and Newt, who were still sunning themselves by the edge of the lake.

As they were leaving, they saw an ice cream parlour, which they couldn't resist.

They each ordered a Knickerbocker Glory as a treat, before setting off on their journey once more towards the famous garden.

Chapter Four

Picnic in Beaurepaire

They drove for an hour or so, until they got into the countryside. Nosferatus' car didn't break down once, much to everyone's relief!

Soon, Nosferatus pulled off the road and parked up beside a farm shop.

"We will get some food for the nicpic," he announced.

They all knew he meant 'picnic', but no one said anything.

They went into the shop and bought bread, cheese, tomatoes, potato salad and lots of other nice things to eat. They found some bottles of fizzy apple juice on the shelf called 'Fizz du Pomme' and put a few bottles in the trolley.

Nosferatus placed a pack of ostrich steaks into the trolley, which he planned to barbeque, so they were in for a fine feast. They got back in the cars and headed off again. Soon they arrived at a little wooden shack in the middle of the woods.

"This place belongs to my cousin," said Nosferatus. "He lets me use it whenever I want."

It clearly hadn't been used for some time, as the garden was overgrown, and the garden furniture was covered in old leaves and green moss. The Fairy Princess was a little bit put off at the thought of having their 'nicpic' there.

However, in the blink of an eye, Madame Craccodile swept the table with a broom and placed a nice clean tablecloth over it. Then she set the table with glasses and cutlery. She walked round the garden and picked a few brightly coloured wildflowers which she put into a vase and placed in the middle of the table. Now it looked fit for a King!

The Grumpy Gnome and Captain Robert built a fire in a brick barbeque and Nosferatus prepared the ostrich steaks for cooking.

Finally, the food was ready, and they all sat at the table and ate their meal. The sun was shining down through the trees and they were bathed in warm, golden sunlight.

When they had finished, they cleared away the picnic things.

Nosferatus lined up some old tins on a wall and got his catapult out. Nosferatus, Captain Robert and the Grumpy Gnome took turns shooting at the tins. The Fairy Princess was playing her ukulele, with First Mate Ron singing along very badly and out of tune. Marko-the-Wisp had fallen fast asleep at the table, snoring in time with the music!

After a while, they decided to go for a walk and headed up an old track which led to the top of a hill. It was a very warm day and when they reached the top of the track they sat down for a rest.

There was a ruin of an old cottage nearby. It was overgrown with ivy and stinging nettles. They had a peek inside and saw piles and piles of old books everywhere. There was also an old armchair, a bookshelf full of more books, and a broken table. A gaudy patterned wallpaper was hanging off the walls and a picture of a black cat was hanging at an angle. The Fairy Princess looked through one of the books which had strange symbols and runes on the front cover.

"I think this is a witch's spell book," she said looking nervously around. "We should leave just in case she comes back," urged the Fairy Princess. They all agreed and left the cottage and walked down the other side of the hill.

After about ten minutes, they came to a clearing with a large pond in the middle. You could only see it when you got up close, as it was surrounded by trees and plants. All around there were dozens of dragonflies and damson flies hovering here and there. The pond surface was covered in water lilies with the odd frog sitting on a lily pad warming itself in the sunshine.

They all sat by the pond for a while drinking 'Fizz du Pomme' and watching the dragonflies. Marko-the-Wisp felt very hot and said, "I'm going to paddle my feet in the pond to cool off."

He rolled up his trouser legs and took off his shoes. Then he stepped into the pond and instantly disappeared under the surface! He quickly re-emerged, spluttering, and coughing, with a lily pad on his head just like a hat!

"That was a bit deeper than I expected," he said breathlessly, clambering back out.

"Don't worry, you'll soon dry off," the Fairy Princess told him.

They made their way back to the wooden shack and prepared their beds for the night. Nosferatus had lit a campfire and they toasted marshmallows to go with the hot chocolate Madame Craccodile had made. The Fairy Princess played her ukulele, and they all had a singsong round the campfire before turning into bed for the night.

The Fairy Princess lay in her bed listening to an owl hooting nearby before she fell fast asleep.

The next morning, they were all up as soon as it was light. Nosferatus cooked everyone breakfast before they set off on the next day of the holiday.

Chapter Five

The Confluence

They drove for a few hours before Nosferatus pulled off the road next to a small restaurant by a huge river.

"This is the confluence," said Nosferatus, "where two great rivers meet and become one," he continued. "We can watch the river for a while, as there are always lots of things happening. One river is called the Saône and the other is called the Rhône. When they join it is just called the Rhône."

The restaurant served fish and chips. Everyone ordered a portion of fish and chips (the cats just had fish) and sat at a table outside, watching the rivers go by on either side as they joined into one.

The chips were delicious, it had been quite a while since they'd had breakfast and they were feeling famished.

After they finished their lunch, Captain Robert, Nosferatus and the Grumpy Gnome held a stone skimming competition. They were all quite good at it, but Captain Robert's went further than the others.

A few years ago, Captain Robert came runner up in the Easedale Island World Stone Skimming Competition in Scotland!

First Mate Ron stood up and asked Captain Robert, "Can you teach me how to do it, please?"

"It's all in the wrist action," he said showing her in slow motion. Then he flicked the pebble and it skimmed and bounced on top of the water before slipping under the surface.

Each time First Mate Ron threw her stone it fell in with a 'plop'!

Captain Robert demonstrated several more times.

"I think I've got the hang of it now," said First Mate Ron and skimmed a stone halfway across the river!

"Do that again!" said Captain Robert.

First Mate Ron found another pebble and skimmed it across the river going even further than the last time! Everyone stood there open mouthed. "I think I have won the competition!" she shouted waving her arms and dancing a funny jig. Captain Robert just raised his eyes to the sky.

Following that they spotted a small fairground and went along to go on some of the rides. First, they got on a Ferris wheel, where from the top you could see for miles and miles.

Next, they saw a brightly coloured carousel with golden horses.

"Let's have a go on that," said First Mate Ron, dashing towards the carousel.

An old man was sitting nearby taking the money for the ride.

"Can we get on, please?" First Mate Ron asked the old man.

"Oui, yes, you can," answered the old man. They all got on a horse each and waited for it to start.

"Would you like slow, quick or frisky?" asked the old man.

Before anyone else could answer, First Mate Ron shouted, "Frisky!" and the ride began. The horses started to gallop as they went round and round on the carousel.

"Wheeee! What fun," squealed First Mate Ron.

Then the horses started bucking, then rearing, and First Mate Ron screamed in fright. The old man was laughing so much he had to hold his sides!

They held onto the horses as tightly as they could until, much to their relief, the carousel came to a stop. They jumped off quickly and, deciding they'd had enough of the fairground, walked away with the old man still laughing to himself.

On the way out, they saw a coconut shy and couldn't resist having a turn. They had three wooden balls each. Everyone missed, until it was First Mate Ron's turn. She threw the first ball and it hit the side of the coconut, making it wobble, but it still stayed in the stand. When she went to throw the next ball, she closed one eye to focus, and her tongue stuck out the corner of her mouth in concentration. The next ball hit it straight on and the coconut fell out of the stand. "I have won again!" shouted First Mate Ron triumphantly dancing her funny jig.

The Grumpy Gnome smashed the coconut on a stone and split it open. The coconut milk spilled onto the ground but they each enjoyed a piece of the juicy flesh.

Following that, they set off again on the next stage of the journey to the famous garden.

Chapter Six

The Gypsy Caravan

They drove for about an hour when Nosferatus pulled off the road into a layby.

"We can spend the night here," he said while mysteriously pulling a torch out of his bag. "Follow me," and he walked a short way until they came to a high hedge.

Hidden behind the hedge was a large, wooden gypsy caravan. It had red and yellow paintwork and a blue roof.

"This belongs to my cousin who lets me use it anytime I like," Nosferatus told them, pulling out a key from under the wheel. He opened the door and pulled the step ladder down. Then he climbed inside and lit a wood burner to warm the caravan up.

Outside, Captain Robert and the Grumpy Gnome lit a campfire to cook sausages for supper.

After supper, they lay on the ground looking up at the stars. It was a beautiful clear night, and they could see millions of stars. Because there were no streetlights in the countryside far more stars were visible than there were in the town. The night sky was beautiful with all the stars twinkling away.

"My favourite star constellation is Orion, the Mighty Hunter," said the Fairy Princess. "Can you see him?" she asked pointing up to the sky. "Those are his shoulders, arms and legs and there is his shield, sword and belt. If you imagine a line between the stars, like a dot to dot, it makes his outline," she continued. "Just by his leg you can see his faithful dog star, Sirius, which is one of the brightest stars in the sky."

"I like the Big and Little Dippers best," said Marko-the-Wisp. "Sometimes they call them the Big and Little Bears, or the Big and Little Plough," he went on. "Look, there they are!" he said, pointing randomly to a patch of sky.

They lay there for a while looking up at the stars, whilst the Fairy Princess gently strummed 'Twinkle Twinkle Little Star' on her ukulele.

"Did you know that the starlight we can see is from the past?" said the Fairy Princess, still strumming softly.

"In the past? What do you mean?" asked First Mate Ron.

"The stars are so far away that it takes years and years for their starlight to reach from there to here," the Fairy Princess replied. "So, the starlight that we are currently looking at is from the past. If one of the stars exploded tomorrow, we would keep on seeing their starlight for a long time after it has gone. The stars have their own cosmic magic!"

Then Madame Craccodile began to tell them about the garden they were visiting the next day.

"In France we call it the 'Palais Idéale'. It was built by a little postman, called Ferdinand, a long, long time ago and it took him his whole life to build," she said. "Every day, Ferdinand walked on his postman's round, with his wooden barrow, collecting interesting stones and rocks. With those stones and rocks, he built and created an amazing palace in his back garden where people from all over the world come to visit," she continued.

"Why did he do all that?" asked First Mate Ron.

"Ferdinand's real life was very poor, sad and miserable. He built the palace in his garden to escape his life inside his imagination," said Madame Craccodile. "He read lots of magazines and newspapers. In his imaginary world, he travelled to many countries and had a happy, rich life. Inside his palace, he recreated the pictures from the magazines as sculptures to represent his imaginary travels and ideal life," she explained.

They turned into bed, all deep in thought about Madame Craccodile's story of Ferdinand, the French postman.

Chapter Seven

Ferdinand, The Postman's Garden

The next day, they got up early and packed away their things. Nosferatus locked up the caravan and put the key back under the wheel.

They set off towards Ferdinand, the postman's garden.

Soon, they knew they were getting near as there were signs by the side of the road directing them towards the garden.

They found a car park and parked the cars next to each other. They all got out stretching their arms and legs, which had become stiff with sitting in the car so long.

There was an arrow pointing 'Palais Ideale'. They were all very excited and walked quickly up the path towards the postman's house.

As they walked past Ferdinand's old house, they saw a bronze statue of him outside. There were crowds of people, who all came to marvel at Ferdinand's wonderful garden.

As they turned the corner of the house, they all stopped and gave a gasp!

As it had only been built by one little postman in his garden, they'd imagined it to be quite small. However, it was enormous, like a real palace. Every wall and surface were decorated with all sorts of pebbles, rocks, shells in little sculptures.

They walked round the outside of the palace looking around in wonder. There were so many things to look at. On the front entrance there were three huge figures with very long legs and arms. There were pillars and columns on either side of the entrance all decorated and adorned. They noticed several gargoyles and other strange looking creatures. There were sculptures of unusual trees and animals everywhere. All around the top there were turrets and towers of various shapes and sizes. In other parts there, were large, ornate arches reaching over the top.

Inside the palace it was like a rabbit warren with passages and stairways leading here, there and everywhere. All the walls were covered in beautiful decorations of leaves, plants, vines, fruits, and vegetables. It really seemed like such a magical place. They walked around inside looking at images of the postman's dreams played out on the walls and ceilings.

They came across a little alcove in the palace storing a small, wooden, old barrow that looked like it might fall to bits if it was moved.

"That must be Ferdinand's barrow," said the Grumpy Little Gnome to the Fairy Princess. They stood and looked at it for a while, imagining the little postman pushing it on his round, day after day, year after year, collecting stones, rocks, and pebbles on his way.

They came to an inscription on the wall which said, 'La Fin d'un Rêve'.

"What does that mean?" asked the Grumpy Little Gnome.

"It means 'the end of a dream'," answered the Fairy Princess wistfully. "This must be when he finished his palace of dreams."

They walked round for a few hours more as there was so much to see. Finally, it started to get late and they headed back to the cars.

Chapter Eight

Back to Beaurepaire...

They drove to Nosferatus' cousin's cabin in the woods to stay overnight, before continuing their journey home the following day.

They set the table in the garden and Nosferatus lit a fire in the firepit as it was getting chilly.

They lit the barbeque and cooked sausages and lamb chops, with salad and French bread to go with them. They sat around the firepit late into the night talking about the amazing garden palace and the incredible little French postman who created it all.

The next morning it was bright and sunny. After they had eaten their breakfast, they decided to go for a walk along the track again before setting off on the journey home.

When they got to the top of the hill, they walked past the tumbledown house. They couldn't resist taking another peek inside.

As they approached the cottage, there was an awful smell like rotten eggs.

"What is that ghastly smell?" said First Mate Ron, pinching her nose.

Then, to their dismay, they saw that a witch really did live there! She was sitting there in the chair reading one of her spell books.

The witch was small and skinny, with greyish coloured skin. She was wearing a huge witch's hat which was far too big for her. Her dull, brown hair was sticking out from under her hat like greasy rats' tails.

She glared up over her book at them.

"What are you doing in here?" she hissed.

"So sorry," said the Fairy Princess. "We didn't realise anyone lived here," she added.

The witch was clearly quite angry about the interruption and started to rise up out of her chair, loudly passing wind as she did so! The smell was unbearable, and they were waving their hands in front of their noses. That explained where the rotten egg stink was coming from!

She pointed a bony finger at them.

"I am Michele Grouchy, the best and wickedest witch in France and I am going to cast a spell to teach you a lesson for spying on me!" she screeched, passing even more wind. "Now, where is my wand?" she added, looking round for it.

Then she paused and pointed to Scoobit and smiled an evil sneer.

"As well as casting a spell, I am going to take your white cat because mine has run away. All of the other witches will be green with envy when they see me with such a handsome cat!" she cackled.

The pong was becoming horrendous! They all slowly edged their way out of the cottage shielding Scoobit behind them.

When they got to the door, the Fairy Princess shouted, "Quick, run for your lives everyone!" holding a hankie over her nose.

They all turned on their heels and ran as fast as they could away from the nasty witch. As it was all downhill, they managed to put a good distance between them and witch Michele Grouchy.

They stopped by the lily pond panting heavily and caught their breath for a few moments, constantly glancing behind them for any signs of the unpleasant hag in pursuit. Much to their relief, there was no sign of her.

"What a disagreeable person, no wonder her own cat ran away from her," said First Mate Ron. "How dare she threaten to catnap our Scoobit. There was no need to be so horrid to us either," she continued crossly. "What on earth does she eat to cause that dreadful whiff?" she asked.

"Probably unwitting passers-by!" said Marko-the-Wisp nervously. "Let's get out of here, just in case she has a broomstick or can cast a spell on us from a distance!"

They hurried back to the cabin to pack their things in the cars. After ten minutes they had loaded up and drove away as quickly as they could.

Chapter Nine

Unfinished Business

They drove for a few hours until they reached Madame Craccodile's house.

They stopped for a cup of tea and then they bid their farewells. "We will see you soon," said Madame Craccodile hugging everyone.

"Au revoir, mes amis," said Nosferatus wiping a tear from his eye.

"What did he say?" asked Marko-the-Wisp.

"Goodbye, my friends," translated the Fairy Princess.

They got into Miss Morag Minor and then set off on the long journey home.

On the way, the Fairy Princess asked the Grumpy Gnome, "Please can we stop off at the Parc du Tête d'Or on the way? I've got something I need to do there."

"I suppose we have time, but we can't stay long," replied the Grumpy Gnome.

At the entrance to the park were huge, ornate botanic glass houses. They all stood with their noses pressed to a window peering in at the many exotic plants and flowers growing inside.

The Fairy Princess spotted a little shop selling snacks and sweets and said, "I'll be back in a minute, I am just going to buy something." They all carried on looking in the window of the glass house.

After a few minutes, the Fairy Princess came back with a bag of monkey nuts.

"I love monkey nuts!" exclaimed the Grumpy Gnome, with Marko-the-Wisp nodding in agreement.

"They are not for you," replied the Fairy Princess. "I'm going to see if I can find my little friend, the red squirrel," she added.

They followed her as she walked towards the small wood where she had seen him previously. "Wait here," she said. "If we all go towards them, they will be scared off."

As she approached the trees, there was a small gathering of red squirrels foraging in the dirt for pine nuts and other tasty morsels. They all scattered when they saw her approaching, apart from one. He stood up on his hind legs and looked at her.

She smiled at him and slowly crouched down putting a handful of monkey nuts on the ground nearby. Then she left, walking backwards so she could watch him. To her delight, he went over to the pile and sniffed them. Suddenly, he did several cartwheels and then two backflips! With that, he gathered up as many monkey nuts as he could carry in his little paws and scampered off out of sight.

They turned away to continue their journey home laughing at the squirrel dance.

Chapter Ten

Return Voyage

After several hours, they reached the ferry port. They drove Miss Morag Minor up the gangplank and boarded the ferry.

The sea was choppy and rough. The waves were huge, and some came crashing over the sides of the ferry. When they went up on deck, the boat was rocking so violently that they were having to run from side to side to keep from falling over!

They found a table inside and sat down. Fortunately, the table and chairs were fixed to the floor, so they could hold on tight.

"I don't feel very well," said Marko-the-Wisp dashing to the bathroom. When he came back, he looked a very strange shade of green.

"You poor thing!" exclaimed First Mate Ron. "I have something to help seasickness," she continued, rummaging through her bag. "Here you are," handing him a bag of crystallised ginger.

"I don't think I could eat anything," wailed Marko-the-Wisp.

"Just suck on a bit at first," said First Mate Ron, gently placing a small piece of ginger on his tongue.

Marko-the-Wisp sucked the ginger for a moment, then he chewed and swallowed it. He turned a lighter shade of green. "Is there any more of that?" he enquired.

"Yes!" said First Mate Ron, shoving the whole bag at him. "Take a few pieces," she added. Marko the Wisp did as he was told and took a handful, which he promptly shoved in his mouth!

"This is marvellous!" he mumbled, chewing a mouthful of ginger. His colour turned back to normal and he no longer felt ill.

Finally, the ferry docked at the port and they drove Miss Morag Minor down the gangplank and off on the final leg of their journey home.

Chapter Eleven

Home

They reached the Grumpy Gnome's cottage by sundown and unloaded all the luggage. The Grumpy Gnome parked Miss Morag Minor in her garage and tucked her up in her red woollen tartan rug.

Dragon was waiting at the door to greet them. "Come in, come in," she said. "I've made you something for dinner," she continued. When they got in, they found that Dragon had prepared a delicious buffet made from her gifts from Wales.

They were all famished and tucked into the food until there wasn't a crumb left!

After they had cleared away the plates and cutlery, they went out the back into the garden. It was quite dark, but in the wood at the back of the garden there was a strange, coloured glow.

"What on earth is that light?" asked First Mate Ron.

"It's been there for a few days," answered Welsh Dragon. I sometimes thought I could hear music but maybe I imagined it

"It looks to me like the Travelling Flower Fairies have come to visit your garden, Grumpy Gnome," said the Fairy Princess. "You are very lucky as they don't visit just anyone. They are very shy and secretive but love to have open air parties. Usually, you only know they have visited because they leave behind a ring of toadstools within a dark ring of grass. They sit on the circle of toadstools singing their fairy ballads, dancing and playing their instruments. Your garden is popular with many visitors these days!"

"Do you think we can go and have a look?" asked First Mate Ron.

"We will have to be very quiet and make sure they don't see or hear us. Otherwise, we will frighten them away," replied the Fairy Princess.

They all sneaked up across the lawn, past the apple tree and into the woods. It was very hard to be quiet as there were a lot of bramble bushes to fight through. They got nearer to the light and could hear a faint magical tune that sounded like musical water drops. A fairy started to sing and she had such a beautiful, pure voice that she could have been a nightingale.

They peered round a tree and, sure enough, there was a circle of toadstools with fairies sitting on top cheering and clapping.

The fairies were tiny, and their clothes resembled flowers. One wore a dress that looked like a thistle, and others like a snapdragon, a daffodil, several various coloured roses, a daisy, a buttercup, there were so many. They looked so much like flowers that if one didn't know differently, one might not even notice they were fairies at all!

There was a small fairy orchestra playing strange shaped flutes, and ukuleles, which delighted the Fairy Princess.

In the background, they could see the fairy's camp of little wooden caravans, a bit like the one they stayed in on their holiday. The caravans were rainbow coloured and festooned with brightly coloured bunting, ribbon, and fairy lights.

Nearby, several little horses were tethered to a tree, munching on oats from their nosebags.

They stood behind the trees spying on the fairy's party for a while and then they returned to the cottage.

Marko-the-Wisp picked up his suitcase and said, "Toodle pip for now. I've had a marvellous time, thank you." With that, he slipped through the gate and disappeared behind the hedge.

"Well, what a splendid adventure that was," said the Fairy Princess to First Mate Ron.

"Yes indeed. It's time for us to go though, the dogs will be pleased to see us," said First Mate Ron. They gave the Fairy Princess, Welsh Dragon, and the Grumpy Gnome a hug goodbye and headed off home.

The Fairy Princess and the Welsh Dragon stayed the night at the Grumpy Gnome's house.

The next morning, the Grumpy Gnome made them each a cup of tea and gave them a slice of Welsh fruit cake left over from Dragon's gifts. Then he went off to work.

When the Fairy Princess and Dragon had finished their tea and cake, they went to have a look at the wood at the top of the garden to see if the Travelling Flower Fairies were still there.

When they got through the brambles they peeked around the tree. The fairies had gone but there was a dark ring of grass dotted with hundreds of toadstools.